WHICH WAY, HUGO?

Written by Morgan Matthews
Illustrated by Susan Miller

Troll Associates

Library of Congress Cataloging in Publication Data

Matthews, Morgan.
   Which way, Hugo?

   Summary: An elephant with sore feet tries flying
like a bird, hopping like a kangaroo. and digging like
a mole as ways of going places; then a turtle gives
him some good advice.
   [1. Elephants—Fiction]   I. Miller, Susan,
1956-   ill.   II. Title.
PZ7.M43425Wh   1986   [E]   85-14132
ISBN 0-8167-0648-4 (lib. bdg.)
ISBN 0-8167-0649-2 (pbk.)

WHICH WAY, HUGO?

Hugo was an elephant. All
elephants are big. But Hugo was
very big. He was the biggest
elephant of all.

All elephants like to eat. They
eat a lot. Elephants are big
eaters. Hugo the Elephant liked
to eat. Big Hugo ate lots and lots.
He was the biggest eater of all.

Where did Hugo eat? He ate in
many places. Hugo ate so much,
he had to keep finding new
places to eat.

Hugo had to go here. He had to
go there. Go! Go! Go! Hugo
was always going some place.

How did Hugo go from place to
place? Hugo the Elephant ran.
He ran on his big elephant feet.

Hugo ran here to eat. He ran there to eat. Running and eating. Eating and running. Run! Run! Run! Poor Hugo!

"Go! Go! Go!" cried Hugo.
"Run! Run! Run! No! No! No!
This must stop!"

Hugo the Elephant stopped.
"My feet are sore," cried Hugo.
"Oh my poor sore feet. Running
makes an elephant's feet sore.
This running must stop!"

No running? No going from place to place? But an elephant must eat. Hugo had to go some way. Which way, Hugo?

"To eat, I must go many
places," Hugo said. "But I will
not run on sore feet. I need a
new way to go."

14

A bird flew by. Hugo looked up
at the bird. The bird flew here.
It flew there. The bird flew from
tree to tree.

"Flying?" said Hugo. "Flying is a way to go from place to place. Flying will not make my feet sore. A bird can fly. Can I fly? I will try."

Up a big tree went Hugo.
Up he went to the tree top.
"Now I will try to fly," Hugo
cried.

Hugo hopped out of the tree.
Did he fly like a bird? Oh no!
Down he went like a big, silly
elephant! Crash!

"Ouch!" cried Hugo. "An elephant cannot fly from place to place. All an elephant can do is crash!"

"I must find a new way to go," said Hugo. "An elephant cannot fly. Flying is for the birds!"

No running? No flying? But an elephant must eat. Hugo had to go some way. Which way, Hugo?

A kangaroo went by the tree.
Hop! Hop! Hop! The kangaroo
hopped on its tail. That is how a
kangaroo goes places. It hops
from here to there.

Hugo looked at the kangaroo.
"Hopping," said Hugo.
"Hopping is a way to go from
place to place. I will try
hopping like a kangaroo."

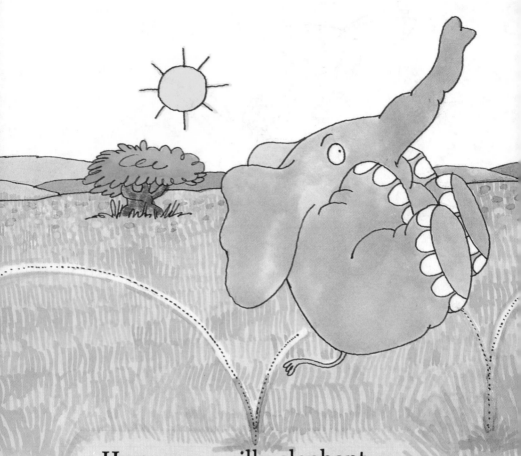

Hugo was a silly elephant.
Kangaroos have big tails. Big
tails are good for hopping.
Elephants do not have big tails.
An elephant cannot hop very
well.

"Hopping will not make my feet
sore," said Hugo. "I will try to
hop. Here I go!"
Hop! Hop! Hop! Up! Down!
Up and down went Hugo
the Elephant.

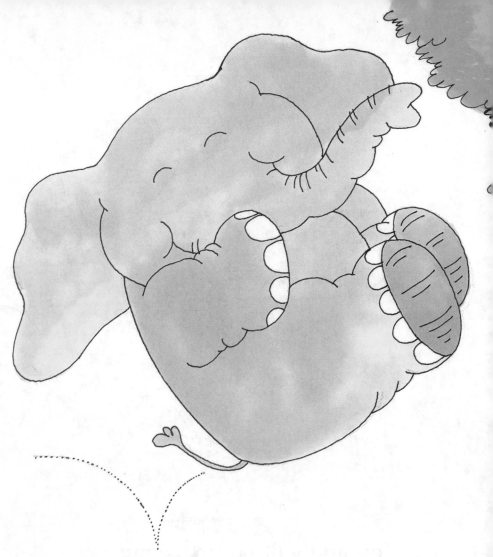

"Look at me!" cried Hugo.
"I'm hopping."
But was Hugo good at hopping?
Oh no! He hopped into things
and onto things.

26

Crash! Crash! Crash!
"Ouch!" cried Hugo. "Hopping
is not good. It makes my tail
sore. It makes me sore. I must
stop!"

Hugo stopped by a tree. Poor, sore Hugo. He was sore from top to tail. What to do? Which way now, Hugo?

By the tree was a hole. In the
hole was a mole. Moles like
holes. Moles dig holes. That is
how a mole goes places. A mole
digs holes.

Hugo looked down at the mole.
The mole looked up at Hugo.
"An elephant!" cried the mole.
"I must go!"

The mole dug a new hole. He
dug and dug. Away he went.
"Look at that mole dig," said
Hugo. "Look at him go."

Hugo looked at the mole's hole.
"Digging holes is a new way to
go," said Hugo. "I will try
digging."

What a silly elephant! Moles are
good at digging holes. Elephants
are not.

But Hugo dug. He dug a hole.
Hugo dug a big hole. The hole
was as big as an elephant.
What a hole!

Did Hugo go places by digging?
No! Down is where he went.
Down! Down! Down! Down in
the hole he went.

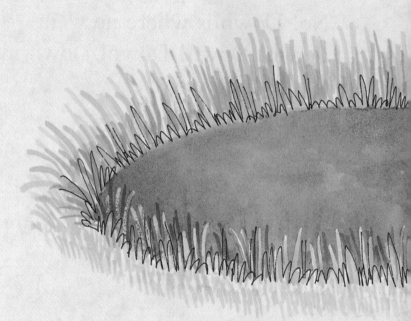

A turtle walked by the hole.
Turtles walk slowly. Slowly, the
turtle walked by the hole. He
looked down in the big hole.
"An elephant in a hole," he
cried. "An elephant digging like
a mole! What a silly thing to do.

"Where are you going, elephant?"

Hugo stopped digging. He
looked up at the turtle.
"I am going no place," said
Hugo. "A mole is good at
digging. An elephant is not."

Up climbed Hugo, out of the hole. Digging was no good. Oh the poor elephant!

"Which way now?" Hugo cried.
"I cannot dig! I cannot hop like
a kangaroo. I cannot fly like a
bird. And I cannot run."

"You cannot run," said the
turtle. "Why not?"
Hugo cried, "I have sore feet."

The turtle looked at the
elephant's feet.
"They do look sore," he said.
"Sore feet are not good. My feet
do not get sore."
"What?" cried Hugo. "How does
a turtle go from place to place?"

The turtle said, "I walk. A
turtle walks slowly. Walking
slowly is good for feet. It does
not make feet sore."

"Walking slowly," cried Hugo.
"That is a new way to go places.
I will try it."

The turtle walked away. He
walked slowly. Hugo walked
away. He walked very slowly.

Hugo walked slowly from place
to place.
"My feet are not sore," he cried.
"Walking is good for poor, sore
elephant feet."

Hugo walked slowly here. He walked slowly there. He walked slowly and ate a lot. His feet did not get sore anymore.

Which way now, Hugo? When
Hugo goes, he walks slowly.